SiDE BY SiDE

Life is better TOGETHER!

Written by Rosie Greening

Copyright © 2021

make believe ideas ltd

The Wilderness, Berkhamsted, Hertfordshire, HP4 2AZ, UK.
557 Broadway, New York, NY 10012, USA.

www.makebelieveideas.com

Everyone **loves** unicorns. They always make a fuss. But you know who **should** be famous?

The unicorns make **rainbows** that **curve** from side to side.

but they make
amazing
slides!

Unicorns sign hoofprints,

Show-off.

and they grant your **wishes,** too.

We don't have
powers like that,

but we still make **dreams** come true!

The unicorns build **palaces** with sweet **marshmallow walls.**

No adoring fans allowed

EEW, unicorn palaces are **gross!**

We have **multicolored** tents

ALL WELCOME

The unicorns **bring sunshine** everywhere they go.

The sun is super boring. You know what's better?

SNOW!

The unicorns are bigheads –
they **show off** all day long.

They **never** want to play with us, and –

HEY!

You've got it wrong.

MANE-GAIN!
Grow luscious locks in minutes

They're not THAT bad…

It's **hard** to be a
unicorn –
we have a **lot** to do.

There's **never**
any time to play.
We wish we were
like **YOU!**

and this is how you sliiiiiiiiide.

Nice rainbow, Ronald!

Everything
is much more fun
if we play side by side!

Everyone is **different**,
but **special** in their way.

So let's **learn** from one another
and have more **fun** every day!